DREAMWORKS

H🌀ME

THE CHAPTER BOOK

Adapted by Tracey West

Simon Spotlight
New York London Toronto Sydney New Delhi

SIMON SPOTLIGHT
An imprint of Simon & Schuster Children's Publishing Division
1230 Avenue of the Americas, New York, New York 10020
First Simon Spotlight hardcover edition February 2015
DreamWorks Home © 2015 DreamWorks Animation LLC.
All Rights Reserved.
All rights reserved, including the right of reproduction in whole or in part in any form.
SIMON SPOTLIGHT and colophon are registered trademarks of Simon & Schuster, Inc.
For information about special discounts for bulk purchases, please contact Simon & Schuster Special Sales at 1-866-506-1949 or business@simonandschuster.com.
Designed by Nick Sciacca
Manufactured in the United States of America 1214 FFG
10 9 8 7 6 5 4 3 2 1
ISBN 978-1-4814-2608-4 (hc)
ISBN 978-1-4814-2606-0 (pbk)
ISBN 978-1-4814-2609-1 (eBook)

CHAPTER ONE

The Boov Mothership rocketed through space, looking like a giant blue ball. The planet the Boov called home had just been destroyed by their enemy, the Gorg, and thousands of tiny Boov were fleeing.

About knee-high to an average human, each Boov had a big, round head and two big, round eyes. Each Boov was a different shade of purple and walked on six stubby legs. The Boov were pretty cute, as aliens go.

But they were not brave.

"Run away!" the leader of the Boov, Captain Smek, ordered every time the Gorg destroyed a Boov planet. He had horns on top of his head and fleshy flaps above his mouth that looked like a mustache. Captain Smek carried a Shusher, a scepter with a rock in the handle that he often used to whack the Boov to make them stop talking. He had taken the rock from the Gorg as a trophy.

The Boov had just fled one of the last planets in the known universe, and their ship was almost out of battery power. They needed a new home, and fast.

"Good news! I has found a planet that the Gorg do not know exists!" Captain Smek said. "It is called Earth . . . for now."

The Boov lined up with their suitcases, ready to go. All of the Boov looked bored except for a Boov named Oh. He hopped up and down with excitement, but the other Boov ignored him.

"We has found the best planet ever forto hiding," Oh said, pointing to a picture on his Boovpad. "The Gorg don't know where it is!"

Captain Smek explained that Earth was inhabited by 'humanspersons,' but assured the Boov that they were not a threat. "My fellow Boov, the humanspersons are backward creatures, but

the Boov will nurture to them, friend to them, and most importantly, relocate them."

Oh turned to another Boov. "We are going to be so good for them," he said. "Is this not excitement?"

"Set a course for our new home!" Captain Smek ordered.

The Mothership sputtered toward Earth, reaching it just as the battery power was nearing zero. Then the Boov turned off Earth's gravity, sending people, animals, cars, and other objects drifting through the air.

"Do not fear, humanspersons! I am Captain Smek, leader of the Boov, and we are simply turning off your gravity temporarily so as to make your mandatory relocation easier, and more fun!" he said with a grin.

Boov Bubble-ships descended to the cities, using huge Foomper Tubes to pick up all the floating humans and relocate them to what the Boov called Happy Humanstown. It was full of things the Boov thought humans loved. There were balloons, fried food, and an amusement park.

"This is gonna be the best vacation of our lives," a man said to a Boov guard.

"Welcome to your new home," the Boov replied.

"Wait—what?" the man asked, shocked.

The Boov just moved on to greeting the next human. "Welcome to your new home," he repeated.

CHAPTER TWO
☉☉☉❂☉☉☉ ☉☉☉

Like most humans, Gratuity Tucci would never for-
get the day the Boov invaded.

For one thing, it was Christmas morning. She and
her mom were opening presents under the tree. It was
just Tip (that was Gratuity's nickname) and her mom,
Lucy, and that's how Tip liked it. It had been that way
ever since they had moved to Boston from Barbados.

Tip was about to give her mom a present when
the Boov turned off the gravity.

"Mom!" Tip yelled.

"Hold on!" Lucy yelled back.

Suddenly, there was a hole in the ceiling, and a big tube came down from the sky. Tip watched, surprised, as the tube picked her mom right up through the hole.

Tip held on, and Pig, Tip's cat, held on to Tip's head. Light swept across the room from a Boov

scanner. Because Pig was sitting on Tip's head like a hat, the scanner only noticed that there was a cat in the room, and reported, "Life form detected. Not human."

Tip stayed where she was until the Boov turned the gravity back on. Peeking out the window, she saw every human in sight being picked up by the tubes. Weird round alien ships floated in the air.

Tip wondered what was happening.

Tip wanted more than anything to go looking for her mom. But she knew she had to stay safe. She and Pig holed up in the apartment.

Mom will find me, she kept telling herself. *She'll come back.*

But her mom didn't come. And then one morning, Tip heard a rumbling and raced to the window. A Boov ship landed on the street outside, and a hundred Boov walked out.

"Sector 195 is ready for occupation," a Boov greeter informed them.

Tip picked up Pig. "We can't wait for Mom, Pig. We gotta go. Now."

She quickly grabbed her phone, keys, and some cans of cat food, and stuffed them into a bag. Then, on an impulse, she grabbed the Christmas present that her mom hadn't opened yet.

Tip snuck outside to the alley, where she had hidden her mom's car under a pile of trash bags. Even though Tip was twelve years old, she had been riding in the front seat long enough to know what to do, since this was an emergency. She and Pig climbed inside. Tip took a deep breath and started the car.

"Let's go find Mom," she said.

CHAPTER THREE
ᑕᕼᗩᑭTᕮᖇ Tᕼᖇᕮᕮ

As Tip made her escape, Oh was happily getting settled in his new home—a building full of Boov settlers. Well, almost happily. One thing made him unhappy: He had no friends.

"You are all invited to my warming of the house party!" he shouted down the hall. "Say, five o'clock?"

"Sure," said a neighbor Boov, in a way that made him sound not sure at all.

Oh wasn't discouraged. He hung a picture of

Captain Smek on the wall, cooked a cookbook until it was nicely toasted, and made a snack by breaking a vinyl record into pieces and serving them next to a can of paint to use as a dip. He put together a tray of glasses filled with motor oil and sandwiches, and waited by the door for his first guest to arrive.

Oh waited, and waited, and waited. Finally, he realized no one was coming.

That's when Oh heard footsteps and thought they might be from a party guest. He went out into the hallway, but no one was there. A neighbor's apartment door was open, so he walked inside.

"Neighbors, hello?" Oh said.

Oh didn't see that some Boov were hiding from him behind a chair. He sighed and gave up, sitting on the balcony and eating a record, all by himself.

That's when he spotted Kyle, a Boov Traffic Cop, on the street below. Oh floated down to the ground

in his Bubble-ship, hopped out, and stood next to Kyle.

"Hello, friend Kyle," he said.

Kyle sighed. "I am not your friend."

"Of course you are! We have had many enjoyable talks," Oh said.

"No, we talk only because I am not allowed to move," Kyle pointed out.

"See, you are always saying funny things," said Oh. "Perhaps you can say them at my warming of the house party tonight."

Kyle shook his head. "I will not. Parties are useless and take up valuable Boov time."

"Well, since you are at your busyness, I shall send you an e-mail invitation so you can join later during your leisure minute."

"Please do not send," Kyle begged. "I enjoy my leisure minute."

Oh pressed a button on his Boovpad. "Fa-da! I have sent directions to my living space."

Chirp! Chirp! Chirp! Suddenly, Boovpads all over the world chirped with an "incoming mail" chime.

Oh looked down at his phone. He had accidentally hit the send-all button.

"You sent directions to everyone?" Kyle cried.

"Uh-oh," said Oh as he looked down at his Boovpad and realized the message had been sent to Kyle and to the rest of the universe. "But no matter. All are welcome to my party!"

"'Uh-oh' is right!" yelled Kyle. "Our enemy, the Gorg, will get it and can use directions forto find us. You have doomed our species!"

"I did not mean to," said Oh. "I am sorry!"

"You are arresting!" Kyle shouted.

Panicked, Oh backed up and stumbled into a Bubble-car. Realizing he had no choice but to speed away, he flew through the streets of Boston, away from the Boov police sirens.

"Autopilot! Takes me to a place with no Boov!" Oh yelled.

"I am sorry. You are Fugitive Boov. Starting self-destruct," the mechanical voice told him.

Poof! The bubble popped open and Oh tumbled

to the ground. He quickly ducked into a convenience store to escape detection.

Oh thought the store was empty. But it wasn't. Tip and Pig were inside. Spooked by the Boov police vehicles, Tip drove to the store to hide.

Tip walked down one aisle. Oh walked down another aisle. Then they both turned a corner. . . .

"Aaaaaaaaah!" screamed Oh.

"Aaaaaaaaah!" screamed Tip.

CHAPTER FOUR

Tip quickly shoved Oh into an open freezer case.

"Gotcha!" she cried.

"What for are you did this?" Oh asked. "I am Boov! Beloved by all humans!"

"I know what you are," Tip said.

"Excellent! Can I come into the out now?" Oh asked.

"No!" Tip replied.

She stuck a broom through the handle of the

freezer case, trapping Oh inside. Then she headed for the exit.

Oh thought quickly. He could not be trapped! The Boov police would find him.

Then he saw Tip's car outside. She had crashed into the parking barrier. Liquid pooled underneath the engine.

"Wait! I can to fixing your car. I seen you has broken it!" he yelled through the glass.

"I did not break it!" Tip said. But when she tried to start the car, nothing happened.

Tip knew she had no choice. She couldn't find her mom without the car. She let Oh out of the freezer.

Tip kept watch for Boov police while Oh fixed the car. He worked fast, and by the time the car was done, it looked really weird. Hoses snaked out

everywhere. And Oh had bolted the slushy frozen drink machine from the store on top of the roof.

"Mom's going to kill me," Tip muttered. She climbed into the car.

"You can drives first," Oh said, walking to the passenger's side.

"You're not coming," Tip said. "I'm trying to hide

from the Boov. I'm not bringing one with me. You'll just turn me in."

"No! I just needs a ride," Oh said. "I haves official Boov business out of town."

"Me too," Tip said. She started the car, and it lit up like a spaceship! Then it started to float above the ground.

"What did you do to my car?" Tip yelled.

"What does you mean? It should to hover much better now," Oh said.

Tip played with the controls until she figured out how it worked. She started to take off when Oh stepped in front of the car.

"Wait! Why for you do this? Humans and Boov are friends!"

"We're not friends," said Tip. "You kidnapped my mom."

Oh was puzzled. "Who is MyMom?"

"No, my *mom*!" said Tip, stepping on the gas again.

"I knows how to find her!" Oh blurted out again. "The information is at Boov Central Command! At the Great Antenna, in the Paris."

"Promise you'll help me get to Paris and find her, or you're not getting in my car!" Tip said.

"I promise!" Oh said as the sound of sirens got closer. "But if you do not wish to be capturing, we must be going now!"

Tip wasn't sure if she could trust Oh, but she didn't want to get caught by the Boov police. She had to decide what to do, and fast!

"Fine. Get in," she told Oh.

CHAPTER FIVE

ᘓᘓᘗᘎᘎᘖᘖ ᘎᘓᖇᘎ

Tip flew the car away from Boston, and together she, Oh, and Pig soared across the night sky. It would take hours to get to Paris, and Tip and Oh talked to pass the time.

"What is your name?" Oh asked.

"Gratuity Tucci," she replied. "But my friends call me Tip."

"Tip," said Oh.

"I said, my *friends*," Tip corrected him.

"But we are friends. All humans and Boov," said Oh. "Captain Smek has decided."

"Captain Smek is an idiot," Tip said.

"Untrue. Captain Smek is a genius and best at running away," Oh said.

Tip rolled her eyes. "What a coward."

"Long ago, our enemy, the Gorg, invited the Boov to a peace meeting, and Captain Smek wisely fled in terror," Oh tried to explain. "He took with him a great trophy called the Shusher."

"Why is it called a Shusher?" Tip asked.

"Because when Boov make mistake, he shushes them by thumping them on the head with it," explained Oh.

"Whatever," Tip said.

"Would you like to knowing my name now?" Oh went on. "I have chosen a popular human name for myself. I am Oh."

"Oh? Your name is Oh?" Tip asked. "Who told you that was popular?"

"Because it is. It is used by many famous humanspersons. There is the 'J.Lo' and the 'Groucho' and the 'Bono,'" he replied.

"Fine," said Tip. "Your Earth name is Oh."

"Not Earth. Smekland." Oh corrected her.

Tip sighed. This was going to be a long trip.

When they reached New York, Tip flew the car to a rest stop. They had started calling the car Slushious because of its frozen drink machine, and parked it under an overhang to avoid being noticed. Then she and Oh got out to stretch their legs and use the bathroom.

"Be out in a second," Tip yelled to Oh. "And then Paris, here we come!"

They had just flown by a bunch of "Wanted" posters with Oh's face on them, but Tip hadn't noticed because Oh distracted her by using a compact mirror to flash light in her eyes. Oh knew that if he went to Paris, he would be captured. The only safe place for him to go was

Antarctica, where there were no Boov to find him.

"Takes your time!" Oh yelled to Tip, panicking. He ran to Slushious, and entered "Antarctica" into the navigation screen.

"Fugitive Boov!" said someone. It was Kyle, and he was standing just outside the window. "Hold still for arresting."

That's when Tip ran out, knocking over a gigantic tower of oilcans, burying Kyle under them.

"You has saved us!" Oh said to Tip.

"You're 'Fugitive Boov'?" Tip asked Oh. "You were going to ditch me! You promised to help me find my mom!"

While they were arguing, Tip and Oh got back in the car. Meanwhile, Kyle stumbled over to them.

"Freezing!" he ordered. Captain Smek wanted Oh's password, so Kyle was determined to get it.

That's when Tip sent Slushious flying straight up. The noise startled Kyle, causing a bubble to hit the gas pumps by mistake, creating a huge explosion.

"Oopsness," Kyle said. He thought Oh was erased forever.

Kyle didn't see that Tip had driven Slushious away just in time. Inside Slushious, Oh's eyes grew wide. Tip had saved him again!

CHAPTER SIX
ⓒⓒⓒⓥⓐⓦⓢ ⋂ⓒⓞ

Powered by Oh's technology and sweet slushy drinks, Tip, Oh, and Pig continued the flight to Paris. While they were flying, Oh explained why he was a fugitive. He told Tip that if his invitation reached the Gorg, the Gorg would find them. But he was sure the Big Brain Boov would figure out Oh's password and intercept the e-mail before it reached the Gorg.

"So, you're a fugitive for inviting these Gorg to a party?" Tip asked. "You are so weird."

"You do not understand," said Oh. "The Gorg are not good. Even when we escapes, they destroys the planet behind us so we can never return."

"So your plan is to just run away?" Tip asked. "Have you ever thought of, oh, I don't know, fixing your mistake?"

"It is a miracle your species is not yet extinct," Oh replied.

By the time they reached Paris, Tip and Oh had a plan. The city was crawling with Boov, and Oh needed a disguise. Tip used her mom's makeup kit to give Oh a whole new look. Powder turned him a slightly different shade of purple. A beauty mark on his cheek was the finishing touch.

Then they hid Slushious on top of a building and headed to the Great Antenna. Tip recognized

it as the Eiffel Tower. The Boov had run the top of the tower through a giant Gravity Ball, and it floated above the city.

As they walked, Oh noticed something on the Boovpads everyone carried: a five-minute countdown.

Oh panicked. "How is this possible? The Big Brain Boov have not yet figured out my password!"

They hopped into a Bubble-vator that took them to the top of the tower, where Captain Smek was ordering everyone to the escape ships.

Oh knew he had to input his password to save the planet from the Gorg, and to have time to find Tip's mom. Tip and Oh found an empty Bubble terminal and jumped in so they could access the e-mail system.

"Thirty seconds to doom. I shall input my password," Oh said. He quickly entered a phrase.

"MynameisOhandCaptainSmekisgreatandanyone whodoesnotthinkthatisapoomp." Then he added the number one.

REJECTED.

"Oh no—caps lock!" Oh cried. He quickly typed it in again as the countdown to doom continued. Five. Four. Three. . . . The words SIGNAL CANCELED appeared on every Boov screen.

"Yes!" Oh cheered. Then he quickly typed some more. "And I have found your MyMom. Lucy Tucci is in the place formerly known as Australia."

"Thank you, thank you!" Tip said, hugging him. "Let's go get her!"

As they headed down in the elevator, Oh added, "Now that I has canceled my e-mail, I can finally come out of the hiding!"

But when the elevator doors opened, Tip and Oh came face-to-face with Captain Smek.

CHAPTER SEVEN

⊙⊙⊙⊙⊙⊙⊙ ⊙⊙⊙⊙⊙

Captain Smek was not happy to see Oh.

"Well, well, well," said Captain Smek, wiping the fake beauty mark off Oh's face. "Fugitive Boov! Did you really think you could escape?"

"He's a Hero Boov!" Tip cried.

Oh looked heartbroken. "No, see, I was just coming to tell you I has fixed my mistake!"

"Yes, but before that, you has made many, many, mistakes," said Captain Smek. "Erase him!"

The Boov got ready to erase Oh.

"Don't do it . . ."

Oh turned. It was Tip! She stood underneath the Gravity-Ball controller that kept the tower afloat.

". . . or I will mess with this gravity thingie!" Tip warned.

"She's bluffing," said Captain Smek. "She could not possibly reach the—"

Tip stood on her tiptoes and grabbed the Gravity Ball.

"Curse you and your human tallness!" Captain Smek cried.

Tip looked at Oh, and he nodded. She knew just what to do. If she moved the ball, the tower would move. She turned the ball upside down, and a rumble shook the tower.

"Run for your lives!" Captain Smek yelled.

The Boov grabbed on to anything they could hold as the tower tipped sideways. Some of them splashed into the river below. Tip and Oh held on tightly—and then fell into an empty Bubble-ship.

They reached Slushious and quickly flew away, leaving Paris behind them. They had a long trip ahead of them—17.9348 hours to Australia, by Oh's calculation.

Oh was deep in thought. So many things had happened. He thought Captain Smek was awesome. But he kept trying to erase Oh. Only one being had ever been nice to Oh—and it wasn't a Boov.

He looked at Tip. "Gratuity Tucci, before we came . . . Captain Smek told us that the humans needed us. We were told the humans were backward. It is what we thought."

He paused. "But I am thinking now . . . that we were thinking wrong. And that Captain Smek is the wrongest. I am thinking the Boov should never have come to Smekland . . . to Earthland. So I am saying the sorry to you, Gratuity Tucci."

Tip smiled and handed Oh the keys. "Call me Tip."

Oh climbed into the driver's seat, and they flew . . . and flew . . . and flew. Over Italy and over Greece. Hours and hours passed. Tip fell asleep.

When she woke up, she looked at Oh. He was asleep, with Slushious on autopilot.

The car passed through clouds, into a blue sky over China.

"Aaaaaaaaaaaah!" Tip screamed.

Boov ships filled the sky all around them!

CHAPTER EIGHT

Oh woke up. "Wait," he said. "The Boov ships are running away. There can only be one reason."

He looked in the rearview mirror. Sleek Gorg fighters zipped down from the sky!

"This makes no sense. I stopped the message. Gorg cannot be finding us!" Oh cried. "There must be some other reason."

A Gorg ship pulled up behind them. A Boov ship turned to attack the Gorg ship. Tip pulled the car

up over the action, but part of the Gorg ship broke off and smacked into Slushious. The containers of frozen drink cracked and the colorful liquid splattered.

"We're losing Grape Escape! We lost Tangerine Twist!" Tip cried.

"If we lose Busta Lime, I cannot control!" Oh yelled.

Slushious lost power. It crashed down into a river below, skipped like a stone, and landed in the thick mud of a riverbank.

They heard a buzzing sound as a Gorg fighter whizzed past them. It crashed in the distance.

Tip had an idea. "Maybe you could take parts from that ship to fix the car."

"No! Boov run away from danger. Not toward it," Oh protested.

"Stop being such a Boov," Tip scolded. "It's our only chance! Come on!"

They climbed up the bank and then approached the downed Gorg fighter. To their relief, they saw that the pilot was a robot drone. Oh rooted around and came out holding a strangely shaped object.

"It is a Gorg Super-chip!" he announced very excitedly. "Slushious will fly again!"

Oh quickly fixed the car and they zoomed off to Happy Humanstown, the human settlement in Australia. When they got there, the sky was filled with fleeing Boov ships. Humans gathered outside, cheering.

Tip ran toward the houses. Oh grabbed her by the arm.

"There is no time," he said. "Come with me to the next planet."

"I'm not going," Tip argued. "My mom is here."

Oh shook his head. "You will never find her. It is one hundred percent!"

Tip shook her head. Then she turned and ran into the crowd. Oh hated to see Tip go. But he was a Boov, and Boov ran away. He jumped on the last Boov Transport ship as it took off.

In the control room, Boov were panicking.

"The Gorg Mothership will be here any minute and we are completely out of power!" Captain Smek said.

That's when the Boov looked up and saw the Gorg Mothership through the front window. It was flying toward them and approaching fast.

As everyone ran to the back of the ship, away from the Gorg, Oh ran to the front to the main control sphere.

"It is Fugitive Boov," yelled a Boov who saw Oh. "He is running toward the danger!"

Then Oh shoved the Gorg Super-chip he had taken from Slushious into the control panel.

Vroooom! The chip superpowered the Boov Mothership. It sped away from the Gorg fighters.

The Boov cheered. Oh explained how he had taken the Super-chip from a downed Gorg fighter.

"He ran to the danger," said a Boov named Toni. "He is like a, a Super Boov!"

"No, no, no! I am Super Boov!" protested Captain Smek. "I invented running away, I have the Shusher, and I am your captain!"

"But you are not a good captain," Oh said. "I used to believe you. But then I met a humansperson who is brave and cares about other humanspersons in a way that we Boov do not care about each other."

"Big deal. I have had enough!" Captain Smek yelled. "Shush!"

He started to bring the Shusher down on Oh, but Kyle used his hand to stop him.

"That is enough shushing!" Kyle said.

"How dare you shush a shushing!" Captain Smek replied, furious.

"Oh is right," said Kyle, ignoring Captain Smek. "We need a new captain. I think it should be Oh!"

He grabbed the Shusher from Captain Smek and thrust it into Oh's hand. The Boov all surrounded Oh. They chanted his name.

"Oh! Oh! Oh!"

Oh had never had so many Boov like him before. He felt happy—until he looked out the window, and saw Earth below. Tip was still down there. And all the humans were in danger.

Oh knew what he had to do.

CHAPTER NINE

◐◖◗◖●◗●◓ ◗◖◓◖

Back on Earth, Tip was ready to give up. She couldn't find her mom. The settlement was just too big. She was sitting down with her back against a building when Oh found her.

"Oh! I can't believe it!" Tip cried.

"You and Pigcat are my friends," Oh said. "And also too: I gave you a promise."

Oh held up his Boovpad to show her the tracking device. A tiny green dot was blinking on a map of

the Happy Humanstown settlement. He had located Tip's mom!

Minutes later, Tip was running down the street into the arms of her mom.

"Oh, Tippy! I thought I'd never see you again!" Lucy said tearfully.

"Oh, Mom! I never would have stopped looking until I found you!" Tip replied.

Seeing Tip and her mom hugging gave Oh an idea. He looked at his Shusher.

"They are still looking," Oh said. "Gorg are not the takers. Boov are!"

The Gorg Mothership was now very close, about to land, and was blocking out half the sky.

"We must demonstrating our affections later," Oh told Tip and her mom. "We still have one problem . . . but I haves a plan."

"Is it a good plan?" Tip asked.

Oh looked at the Shusher in his hand. "I does not know. But I have hopes."

Tip, Pig, and Lucy piled into Slushious. But instead of getting in, Oh locked them inside.

"I am sorry," Oh explained. "Tip cannot come into the out now. I am fixing my mistake."

"Please don't do this by yourself," Tip pleaded.

"I am sorry. This is too dangerous," he said. He took a Gravity Ball from his fanny pack, turned a dial, and tossed it into the air. It surrounded the car with Tip, Lucy, and Pig inside, and floated into the sky.

Oh marched toward the huge Gorg ship. The ship was miles long and a mile high. It touched down and wicked-looking massive prongs churned under it, kicking up sands and high winds. At the top, a tiny window stuck out.

"Yes! It is the control deck!" Oh cried. "We can shows the Gorg we has their rock."

Holding the Shusher high, Oh climbed onto a pile of rocks. He had to get the Gorg to see him some-how. But the huge ship rumbled forward, tearing up the earth as it moved.

"Goooorg!" Oh yelled, waving the Shusher.

Tip and her mom floated above the scene in the Gravity Ball.

"They're not gonna see him!" Tip cried. "It's not gonna work!"

Suddenly, she got an idea. She grabbed the Christmas present from the back of the car—the one her mom hadn't opened yet. "Open it!" Tip yelled. "Merry Christmas!"

Lucy unwrapped a mirror that said WORLD'S BEST MOM on it. Tip grabbed it and stood up, holding it up through the sunroof. Then she moved it so it caught the light of the sun. First she shone it on Oh, then the control center, then back to Oh. . . .

There was a loud groaning sound as the Gorg ship started to slow down.

"They see him. It worked!" Tip yelled.

But the ship kept moving closer and closer to Oh. He bravely stayed on the rock, holding up the Shusher.

"It's not going to stop in time." Lucy realized.

Tip panicked. She started pushing against the walls of the Gravity Ball. "Mom, help me with this thing!"

Pushing as hard as they could, they turned the Gravity Ball toward Oh. The Gorg ship moved closer and closer. With the Gravity Ball near the ground, Tip slid down and ran toward Oh.

"Oh! Run!" Tip yelled.

Oh realized that he couldn't get away in time, and threw the Shusher to Tip.

In seconds, the ship swallowed Oh!

Still holding the Shusher, Tip buried her face in her hands. Her mom jumped down from the Gravity Ball and took her daughter in her arms.

Then they heard it.

Beep . . . beep . . . beep.

The ship was backing up! It had sailed right over Oh, but it hadn't crushed him. He was alive!

CHAPTER TEN

ↄↄↄↄↄↄↄↄ ↄↄↄ

Tip ran to hug Oh. Then the massive doors of the Gorg ship opened up and a huge Gorg stepped out into the sunlight. Oh and Tip gazed up at its menacing face, and Oh held up the Shusher.

The Gorg's face began to slowly peel away, revealing a tiny being standing inside the Gorg's head. That's when Oh realized that the tiny being was the real Gorg! The big Gorg was just a suit.

The small Gorg climbed down the suit and stood

face-to-face with Oh. The Gorg took the rock and opened it up. Inside, Oh saw what must have been millions of impossibly tiny dots.

The Gorg spoke to him in Gorg language. Oh answered. The Gorg spoke again and bowed to Oh, then climbed back into the suit and marched onto the ship, with the rock in hand.

Lucy and Pig joined Oh and Tip.

"What was that all about?" Tip asked.

"It turns out Gorg was not here because of my invitation," explained Oh. "Gorg was tracking the rock."

"What was in that thing?" Tip asked.

"Gorg family," Oh replied. "Millions of eggs. It is entire next generation."

"No wonder they've been chasing you," Tip said.

"Not they," said Oh. "She. Apparently that Gorg is last Gorg. That is why rock was so important."

The Gorg ship lifted off, sailing away into the blue sky. The grateful humans gathered around Oh and cheered.

"Thanking you! Thanking you!" said Oh, high-fiving the humans. His heart felt bigger than the Gorg ship.

Soon, Oh decided to throw another warming of the house party. It couldn't have been more different from his first attempt.

This time, he wasn't alone with a bowl of record chips and glasses of motor oil. This time, his home was full of human friends, Boov, and alien friends from all over the galaxy. Oh had finally found friends, a family, and a home, and he would never run away again!

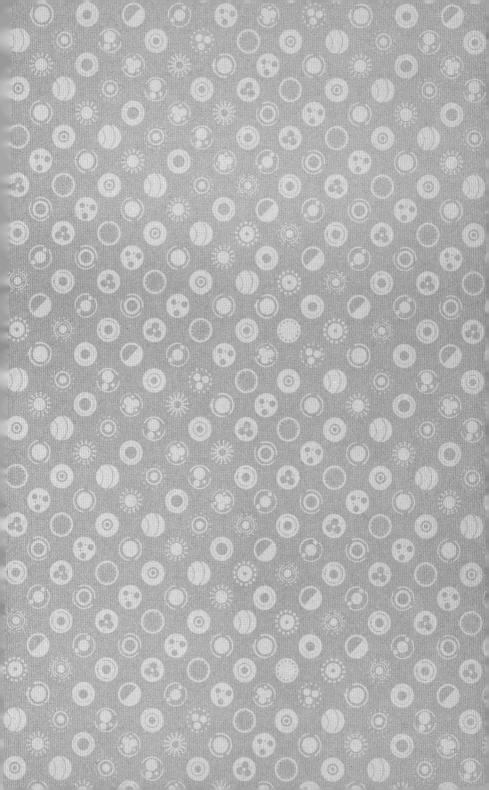

ABOUT THE AUTHOR

TRACEY WEST is the bestselling author of more than two hundred books for children. In addition to writing many media tie-ins, she is the author of the Pixie Tricks series and Dragon Master series. Her home is in New York's Hudson Valley, where she lives with her husband, three stepkids, and their pets.

Be sure to check out these other DreamWorks HOME books!